In the waters off Misty Island, a tour guide was steering a glass-bottomed boat. "You'll find many kinds of fish around Misty Island . . . " he was saying.

A tourist interrupted. "Excuse me, but where are the fish?"

"That's funny," said the guide. "There are usually lots of fish around here."

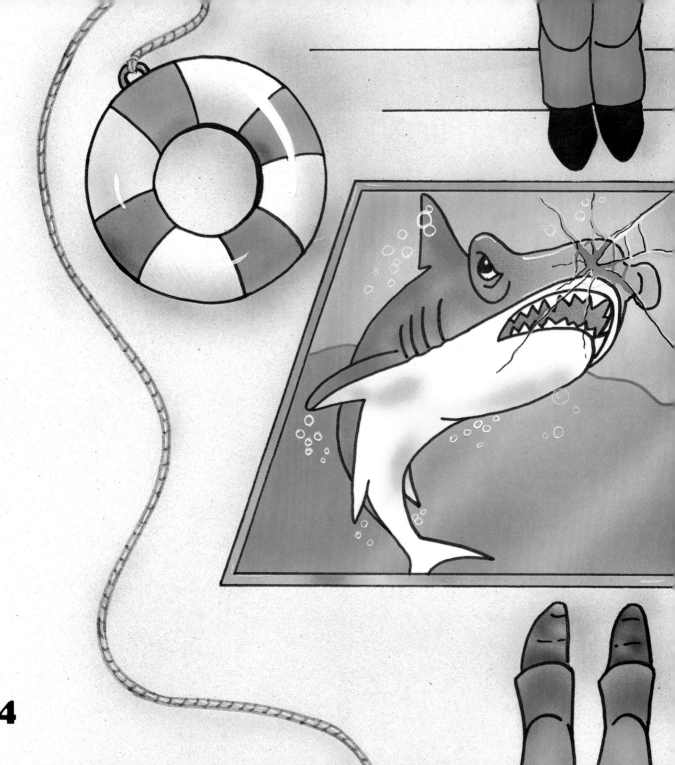

THE SHARK MASTER

**BASED ON EPISODES OF THE NEW ANIMATED SERIES
FROM WARNER BROS.**

**ADAPTED BY ANN MARTIN
ILLUSTRATED BY SEAN GLOVER**

SCHOLASTIC INC.

New York Toronto London Auckland Sydney

ISBN 0-590-25961-X

Copyright © 1995 by Warner Bros. Inc.
All rights reserved. Published by Scholastic Inc. by arrangement with Warner Bros. Inc.
Free Willy, characters, names and related indicia are trademarks of Warner Bros. © 1995 Warner Bros. Productions Ltd., Monarchy Enterprises B.V., Le Studio Canal+.

Book designed by N. L. Kipnis

12 11 10 9 8 7 6 5 4 3 2 1   5 6 7 8 9/9 0/0

Printed in the U.S.A.   24

First Scholastic printing, September 1995

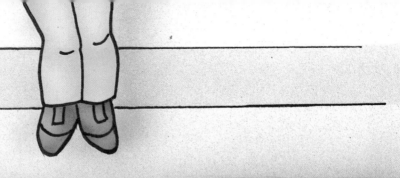

Another tourist pointed at the glass. "What's that?" he cried. A shark was swimming straight for the bottom of the boat.

"That's a hammerhead shark!" shouted the guide. "And I think it's going to . . . "

CRASH! The shark smashed into the viewing glass. Water sprayed through the cracks.

The guide grabbed the wheel and sped back toward the island. "I think we've seen enough for one tour," he gasped.

At the Misty Island Oceanographic Institute, Marlene, a marine specialist, was hanging up the phone. "That's three shark attacks reported today," she said to Randolph, the manager of the institute.

"There have never been three attacks reported in a year, let alone a day!" he said. "It's a bad time to be in the water."

They both had the same thought at the same time. "Oh, no! Jesse!" they exclaimed together.

Lucille the sea lion, who lived at the institute, was goofing around in the water with Jesse. Suddenly Jesse's face became serious. He pointed. "Is that a shark behind you?"

Lucille looked behind her and barked in surprise. "Hurry, hold onto me and swim!" she cried. Lucille towed Jesse toward shore as fast as she could.

Marlene and Randolph were waiting on the
dock. They pulled Jesse to safety, and Lucille
dove underwater. The shark was still after her.
No matter what she did or where she went,
she couldn't get away.

The shark had her pinned against the rocks
when . . . WHAM! The shark was knocked away.
It was Willy! "Mind if I butt in?" he said.
The shark raced away.
Lucille sighed with relief. "Let's go home,"
she said.

Meanwhile, in the deep ocean, a large group of different kinds of sharks were hungrily following a submarine. And inside, the evil Machine was talking to his amphonids, mutants he had created and now controlled. "Release more shark bait!" he ordered.

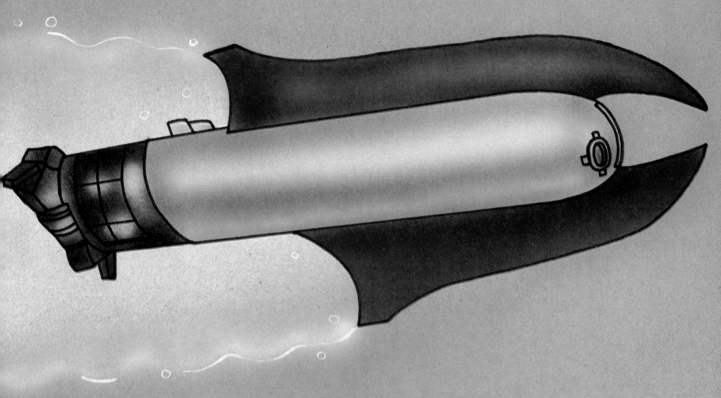

"After we've led this group to the baiting station, we'll go back to sea for more. My baiting station will keep the waters off Misty Island full of sharks. Soon, all the tourists will be scared away. Then, when I start drilling for oil, no one will try to stop me."

Back at the institute, Jesse and his friends were trying to figure out why there were so many sharks in the water. Finally Jesse said, "Well, maybe I should just ask the sharks."

"You mean 'Truth Talk' to them?" asked Marlene. "Great idea! And I know how you can get close to a shark without getting hurt."

Later that day, the group boarded the institute's research boat. Jesse put on his scuba gear and his radio. Then he climbed into a steel shark cage. As the cage was lowered into the water, Randolph threw chunks of fish into the sea. Soon the first sharks began to appear.

Jesse tried to calm himself as a tiger shark swam up to the cage. "Calm down, breathe, focus," he said to himself. Then he tried talking to the shark. "Do-you-understand-me?" he asked.

The shark grabbed the cage with his teeth and thrashed its huge body. Then he disappeared into the dark water.

Jesse spoke into his radio. "He seemed to understand me, but he didn't answer. I guess sharks can't talk."

"Can talk!" boomed a voice behind Jesse. He turned and saw a smaller leopard shark behind the cage. "Don't like to!" the shark went on. "Slash talk for food!"

"Slash — is that your name?" asked Jesse. "Randolph!" he said into the radio. "Send down more fish!"

While Slash ate greedily, Jesse asked, "Why are there so many sharks in the water?"

"Smell in water. Smell of prey all around," answered Slash. "Too many sharks!" he gulped. "Eat my food! Try to eat me!"

"Where does the smell come from?" asked Jesse.

"Grounder place," said Slash.

"Grounder place? You mean a human place? Where is it?" insisted Jesse. "If you take me there, you'll have all the food you want."

At the Healing Pond, Jesse told Lucille, Willy, and Einstein, the dolphin, his plan. He would follow Slash to the source of the smell. "But you can't trust any shark! It's too dangerous," Lucille said angrily.

But Jesse insisted. "If we don't do something about the sharks, all the tourists will be gone for good!" He grabbed his camera. "And besides," Jesse added, "I promised not to bring along humans, but I didn't say anything about Willy."

Later, Jesse and Willy followed Slash toward the Machine's baiting station. Suddenly a blue shark swam in front of them. He eyed Jesse hungrily. "Share food?" the blue shark asked Slash.

Willy swam up to him, nose to nose. "Hey, blue shark," he said. "How'd you like to be a black-and-blue shark?" Scared, the blue shark swam off.

19

The Machine was giving orders from his submarine.
"Are you continuing the baiting?" he asked the amphonids at the baiting station.

"Yes, sir," answered an amphonid.

"Be careful!" shouted the Machine. "Too much bait will throw the sharks into a feeding frenzy!"

"Sir," said another amphonid. "There seems to be something bigger than a shark out there."

The Machine looked up at his screen. "It's that whale and his boy! They're spying on me!" he shouted. "Go out there and stop them!"

"But the water is full of sharks," said the amphonid nervously.

"GO!" the Machine ordered.

Slash had stopped just outside the baiting station.
"Big trouble," he said. "BIG!"

Jesse looked up to see a great white shark swimming
toward them.

Willy blocked the shark's path. "Beat it, bully boy!
They're with me!" he warned.

The huge shark swam away.

23

"Danger!" cried Slash. The great white was swimming down from above them.

Willy sped upward toward the shark — SMACK! They collided. But the shark recovered fast. And he swam straight toward Jesse.

"Willy! Help!" cried Jesse.

Willy slammed straight into the shark from behind. "Eat sand, shark!" he laughed. The great white was stuck in the sandy sea floor.

"Way to go — " Jesse started to say. Suddenly he was grabbed by two amphonids. "Huh?! Help! Willy!" he cried.

25

But Willy was busy with the freed great white. Willy took off for the ocean surface. He leaped out of the water. And he came down just as the great white reached the surface. "Sorry to just drop in like this," said Willy. He crashed into the great white.

The shark plunged down through the water, out of control. CRASH! He slammed into the roof of the baiting station. The bait release pipe snapped off.

"All the bait is escaping," cried the amphonids, letting go of Jesse. Green chemicals were gushing into the sea. And the sharks were starting to close in.

"Danger! The hunger — too strong!" Slash said to Willy. "Take the grounder away now!"

Willy raced away with Jesse on his back.

When they were safely out of the way, Jesse and Willy looked back at the baiting station. "The sharks are going into a feeding frenzy!" cried Jesse.

Dozens of sharks were smashing against the observation window.

"Swim for your lives!" yelled the amphonids as the sharks broke through the window.

"Those goof-off gobs of goo overbaited the sharks!" screamed the Machine. But there was nothing he could do except watch his baiting station fill with water.

29

A few days later, Lucille and Jesse sat by the Healing Pond. Willy relaxed in the water nearby. "I haven't seen a shark in days," Lucille said happily. "And all the tourists are back."

"I'll never be able to prove it was the Machine who lured all the sharks to Misty Island," said Jesse. "I lost the camera in the fight." He picked up a bucket of fish and headed for the boathouse.

"Where are you taking that?" Willy asked.

"I promised the institute's best fish to Slash for a month," replied Jesse. He tossed Willy a small fish. "I'm afraid you get the leftovers, bud."

With one small flick of his tail, Willy soaked Jesse and Lucille with water. "Never did like sharks," he muttered.